The Cardboard Piano

By Lynne Rae Perkins

 GREENWILLOW BOOKS
An Imprint of HarperCollins*Publishers*

Debbie and Tina both had older sisters.
Their sisters were friends, too.
But they're not in this story.

Debbie and Tina both had dogs.

Tina's dog, Putsi, lifted up off the ground when she barked.

woof

Debbie's dog was called Jimmy.

But their dogs aren't in this story, either.

They both had mothers and fathers, but they're not in this story. Well, they're in it a little bit.

Teeeeenaaaahh!

Dehhh-beeeee!

For the friends and neighbors of my childhood

The composer who practiced on a silent keyboard in his stateroom while crossing the Atlantic Ocean was Sergei Rachmaninoff. The "new song he made up" was his Concerto No. 3 for Piano and Orchestra in D minor, Opus 30.

The Cardboard Piano. Copyright © 2008 by Lynne Rae Perkins. All rights reserved. Manufactured in China. www.harpercollinschildrens.com
Pen and ink and watercolor paint were used to prepare the full-color art. The text type is Candida.

Library of Congress Cataloging-in-Publication Data. Perkins, Lynne Rae. The cardboard piano / by Lynne Rae Perkins.   p. cm. "Greenwillow Books."
Summary: When Debbie tries to interest Tina in playing the piano by creating a cardboard keyboard, not only does it not have the same appeal but they realize they do not need to share everything to be best friends.   ISBN: 978-0-06-154265-7 (trade bdg.) ISBN: 978-0-06-154266-4 (lib. bdg.)
[1. Best friends—Fiction. 2. Friendship—Fiction. 3. Piano—Fiction.] I. Title.   PZ7.P4313Car 2008 [E]—dc22 2007039194

First Edition 10 9 8 7 6 5 4 3 2 1   Greenwillow Books

This story is about Debbie and Tina, who were friends.

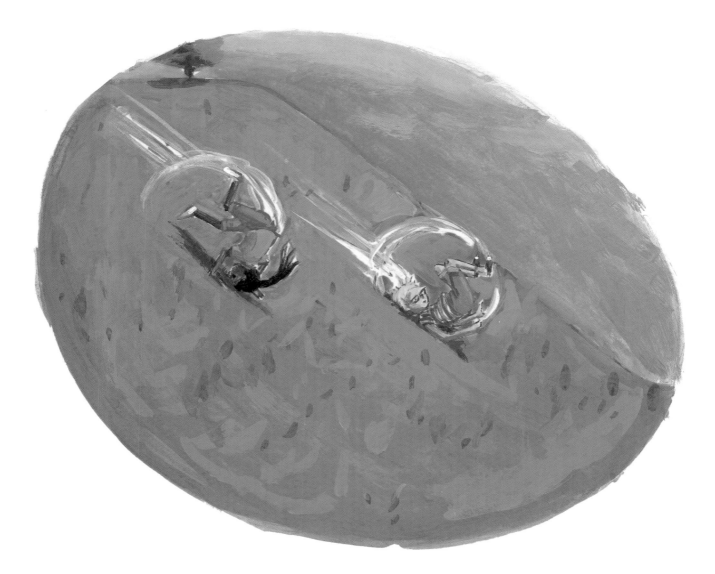

Best friends.

In a lot of ways,
they were alike.

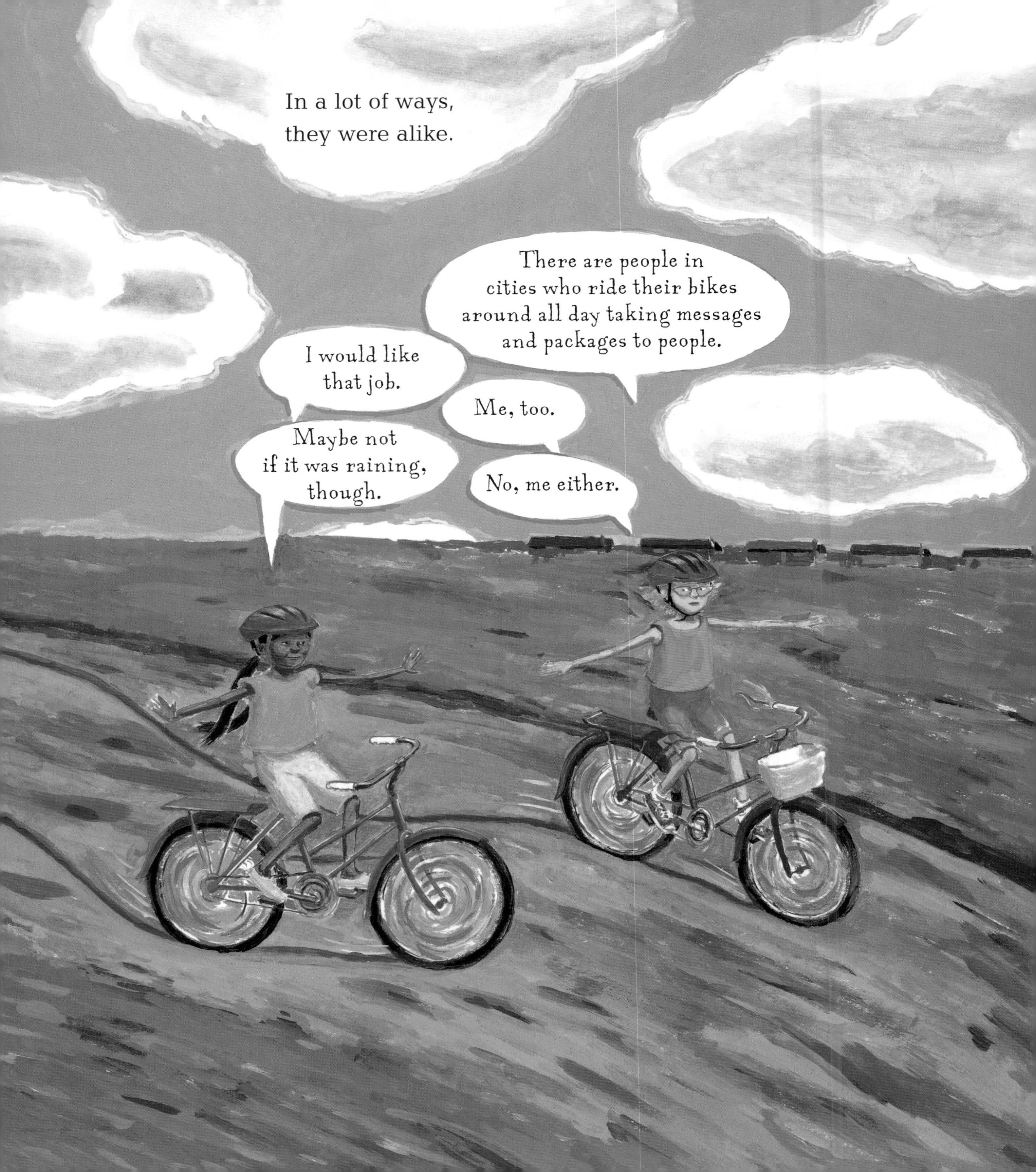

And in some ways,
they weren't.

aahh water floating sun nice happy with my friend

While holding her breath (longer than anyone), she would find the giant pearl. It would be so amazing.

Mostly it evened out.

But Debbie was learning to play the piano,
and Tina wasn't.

Every day, while Debbie practiced for half an hour,
Tina played jacks out on the porch.

And every day, when Debbie came outside again,
Tina would say,

Debbie wanted them both to have piano music.
But she didn't know how it could happen.

Then one day at her piano lesson, Debbie's teacher told her
a true story about a famous musician from the olden days.

He lived in Russia. He was going to travel to America for the first time, and he wanted to write a new song to play when he arrived.

Excuse me, sir, but it is time to go to America now.

He was so busy writing the new song that he forgot to leave time to practice.

So all the way across the Atlantic Ocean, he stayed in his little room on the ship

and practiced on a pretend piano that didn't even make any sound. He could hear the music in his mind.

Listening to the story of the musician from the olden days gave Debbie an idea.

As soon as she got home, she got out some pieces of white cardboard she had been saving.

Carefully, she cut them to the right size.

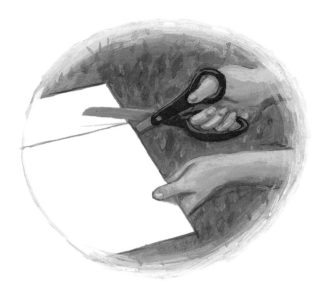

Holding them up to the real piano, she marked where
the keys should go. She drew the straight lines with
a black marker and a ruler, and with the marker,
she colored in the black keys.

She taped the pieces together
as she finished them.

It took a long time, but it
was perfect. It looked
exactly like a real piano.

She could hardly wait
to give it to Tina.

Tina was surprised.

Debbie gave her a lesson on the real piano. It was the same first lesson her piano teacher had given her. When Tina went home that day, she took the cardboard piano with her.

As Debbie practiced that week, she thought about how Tina was practicing, too.

She imagined the two of them playing together. This was called "duets." If they wanted to, they could even sing along.

It was going to be so amazing.

Debbie couldn't believe it.

A day or so later, Tina knocked on the door.
"My mom was cleaning my room," she said.
"She told me to give this back to you."

Tina said, "I tried to hear the notes in my head, but I didn't hear anything. Maybe it was different in the olden days.

"But it wasn't very fun. So I didn't do it anymore."

Debbie watched Tina go back across the street to her own house.
Then she carried the cardboard piano back to her room.

What about how hard she had worked to make it?
What about how they were going to play the piano together?

Maybe Tina just didn't care about doing beautiful wonderful things.
But Debbie knew that wasn't true.

She and Tina did wonderful beautiful things together all the time.

Or maybe Tina just didn't care about trying hard and being amazing.
But Debbie knew that wasn't true, either.

The two of them had difficult, amazing adventures practically every day.

Maybe there was something wrong with the cardboard piano.
Maybe she hadn't made it right.

Debbie hadn't actually tried it out, and she decided to play a song on it. One that she knew by heart. She sang along. She tried it for a while, but all she could hear was her own voice.

"Oranges and lemons," say the bells of St. Clement's . . .

How did that guy in the olden days do it? she wondered. Maybe that's why he was so famous, because he could hear something that wasn't there.

Debbie went to the real piano and sat down. It sounded a lot better.

Debbie thought about how
it was fun to make a tent
out of a bedspread.

A field could be a faraway
country, or another planet.

You could spread mud on rocks
and it was just like putting
icing on cookies.

But it's not that much fun to play a cardboard piano.
The best part isn't there.

The rain had stopped, and there was probably good mud in
the muddy spot.
But Debbie felt like eating real cookies, with real icing. She
wondered if Tina felt like that, too. She decided to find out.
It turned out that Tina felt just the same way.

After they made some, her mother gave Debbie and Tina a plateful
to take over to their neighbor, Mr. K. He was out in his garden.

The cookies reminded Mr. K. of weddings in the land where he grew up. He told Debbie and Tina how people wore ribbons on their hats and their sleeves, and wreaths of flowers on their heads. They sprinkled flower petals on the ground.

As they learned to do the dance, and sing the song, Debbie thought of how they could find ribbons in her mother's present-wrapping box.

They could make wreaths out of clover for their heads.

They already had the right kind of cookies.

They would sing the song and do the dance far into the night, or until the streetlights came on and they had to go inside.

It was going to be so amazing.

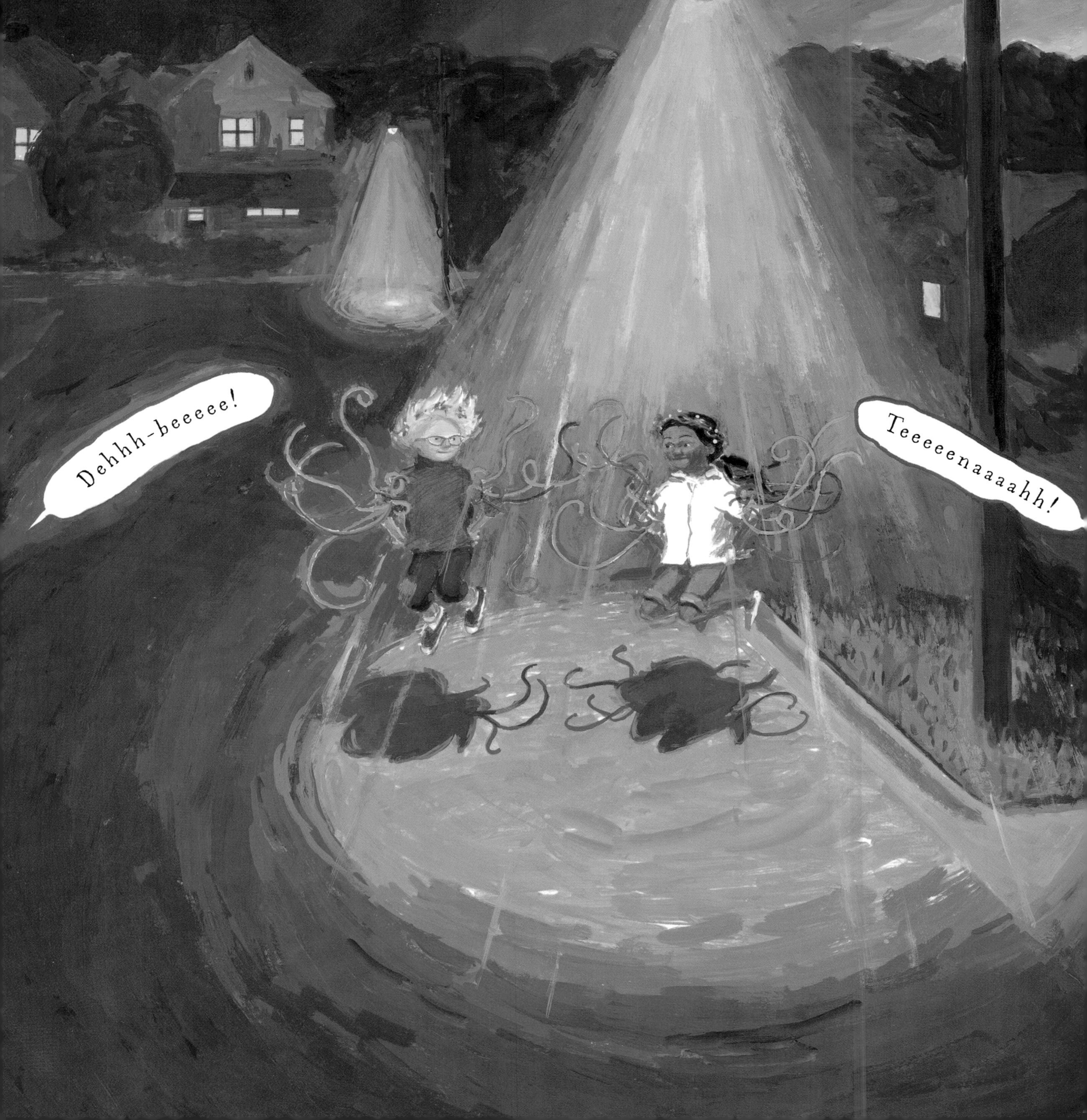

my dog, my cat

Ashlee Fletcher

Tanglewood - Terre Haute, IN

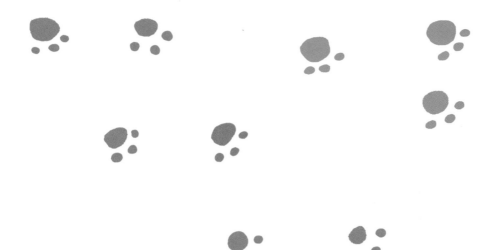

Published by Tanglewood Publishing, Inc., 2011.
© Ashlee Fletcher 2010

Designed by Amy Alick Perich

Tanglewood Publishing, Inc.
PO Box 3009
Terre Haute IN 47803
www.tanglewoodbooks.com

Printed by Worzalla at Stevens Point, WI, in 2010. First printing.
10 9 8 7 6 5 4 3 2 1

ISBN 978-1-933718-22-4

Library of Congress Cataloging-in-Publication Data

Fletcher, Ashlee.
   My dog, my cat / Ashlee Fletcher.
      p. cm.
   Summary: A child points out the differences between a dog and a
cat, but finds something they have in common, as well.
   ISBN 978-1-933718-22-4 (alk. paper)
   [1. Dogs–Fiction. 2. Cats–Fiction.] I. Title.
   PZ7.F62755My 2011
   [E]–dc22
                              2010032919

my dog, my cat

**To
Kennedy and Jack-Jack
my dog, my cat**

I have a dog...

and I have a cat.

Sometimes my dog and

my cat are very different.

My dog barks.

My cat meows.

My dog likes steak.

My cat likes tuna.

My dog's tongue is wet.

My cat's tongue is rough.

My dog likes to chew bones.

My cat likes to chew catnip.

My dog likes to play fetch.

My cat likes to chase yarn.

My dog likes to be wet.

My cat likes to stay dry.

My dog likes to be dirty.

My cat likes to be clean.

**My dog goes to
the bathroom outside.**

**My cat goes to
the bathroom inside.**

My dog likes to dig down low.

My cat likes to climb up high.

Sometimes my dog and my cat

are not very different at all.

My dog and my cat both

love pepperoni pizza!

And my dog and

my cat both love ME!

The End

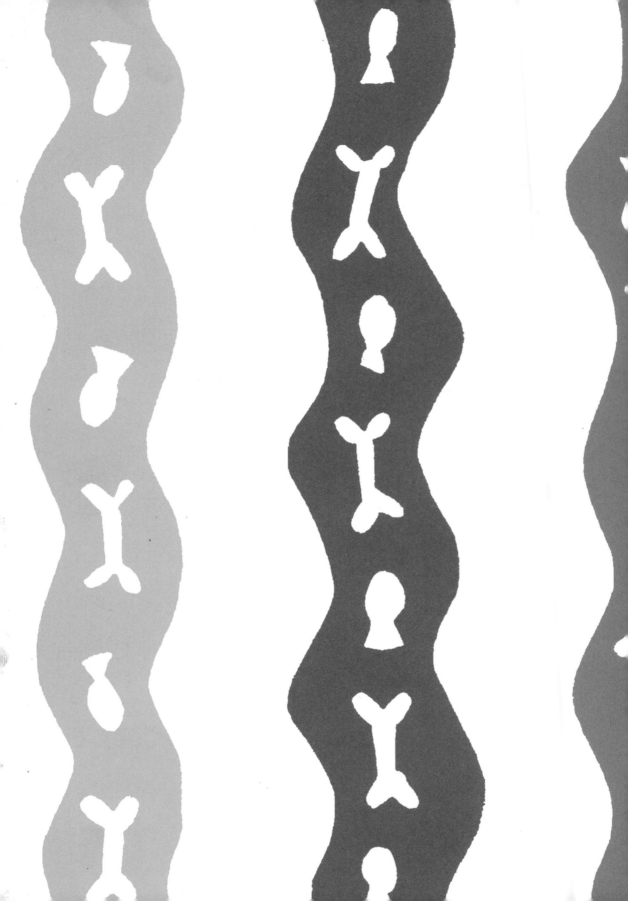